LEO AND THE MAGIC FOREST

EXCITING AND INSPIRATIONAL STORIES FOR BOYS ABOUT COURAGE, SELF—ESTEEM AND INNER—STRENGTH

KATE BURNELL

ISBN – 9798720939489

THIS BOOK BELONGS TO

_____

TABLE OF CONTENTS

LEO AND THE TIMID TROLL

Leo woke from a good night's sleep, stretching as the sun peeked through his curtains. He and his family had just moved into their new house: a gorgeous red-brick building that stood on the edge of a lush green forest. Being nearly ten and very curious, Leo was desperate to explore the forest to see what wonders would be waiting for him. With a sudden jolt of excitement, Leo sprang into action, forcing on his favourite t-shirt and jeans before running down the stairs. He snatched his blue hoodie from the bannister and shoved his feet into his trainers before running through the house towards the front door.

"Leo!" It was his mother, who popped her head from inside the kitchen, smiling at him. "Don't forget your breakfast before you go out, Sweety!" Leo groaned, his hand grasping the front door handle.

"But Muuuuum!" He wailed, "I'm not hungry!" His mother tutted before beckoning him over with a strict finger. He stamped his foot before storming into the kitchen.

"Just have *something*, Leo," she scolded, pushing the fruit bowl in his direction. Leo sighed as he grabbed an apple. He chomped into the juicy fruit and he glared at his mother who nodded, smiling sweetly.

"Don't forget that we are seeing your great Aunt Matilda this evening. I want you back before teatime." She waved a wooden spoon in his direction as she stopped stirring the gloopy porridge on the stove.

"Ahh Muuuuum!" Leo moaned, "I don't like Aunt Matilda! She smells funny!" His mother put her hands on her hips, frowning at her son.

"Everyone is different Leo, you need to show a little kindness." Leo shrugged and walked away, dumping the rest of the apple core into the kitchen rubbish bin before trotting back towards the front door.

"Stay safe, and remember: back for teatime!" Leo waved a hand towards his mother as he sighed to himself before opening the front door.

The dark forest loomed ahead over the red-brick house as he walked down the garden path. The feeling of excitement and curiosity welled up inside him once again.

He followed a path that led into the forest, and it wasn't long, before he noticed a spooky side path. The track was just an animal trail that forked off from the main footpath, deep into the shadows of the trees. He followed the trail and began to feel that he was being watched. Leo shivered as he thought he heard whispering behind him, and as he whirled around he saw… nothing! No one was there.

After some time he leant against a large oak tree and felt something odd digging into his back. Turning to inspect the tree, he saw a smooth circular shape that looked like a…

"A doorknob?" He whispered to himself. Sure enough, as he stood back to look at the tree he saw the faint outline of a small circular door with a smooth handle. It was camouflaged so well that he wouldn't have noticed it if he had just been walking by. Curiosity overcame him, and Leo reached out and turned the strange little doorknob, stooping down to walk through the small door.

Leo stepped through the tree-door, and inhaled sharply as he took in his surroundings. All around him he saw the forest, and he heard in the air the faint sound of chimes jingling softly somewhere in the distance. Beautiful multi-coloured wildflowers covered the forest floor, and the sound of birds could be heard. Leo closed the small door before walking down a path that led from the tree, gobsmacked at the beauty of this place.

He walked through the forest, hearing the leaves of the trees high above him whispering in the wind.

"What *is* this place?" Leo said to himself. Just then a voice sounded behind him, it was deep and gruff.

"This is Magic Forest!" Leo spun around on the spot before falling over in shock at the person standing before him. Underneath the shadow of the trees loomed a dark figure, and as it stepped into the light Leo saw two massive tusks sticking out from its jaw.

Leo stared in horror, before yelling in fear.

"AHHHHHH! A m…m…monster!" Leo scrambled to his feet, before he began to run as fast as he could. He heard the galumphing sound of the monster behind him as he chased him, but soon enough Leo skidded into a dead end. He had stopped in a clearing where stinging nettles grew around the edge of the clearing, with no way to escape. He turned around as he wondered what to do, certain he was about to be eaten as the monster stamped into the clearing. Leo yelled again as a shaft of light showed the monsters' features.

The monster was covered in a thick brown fur that covered its whole body with long black claws that grew from hands as large as a dish. Leo backed up against a tree, shaking.

"P…p-p-please don't eat me!" Leo begged. The monster stopped walking, and began to… *cry*. Its sobs echoed all around.

"I'm not trying to eat you! I'm a vegetarian!" The beast wiped his snotty nose on his furry arm. "I just want a friend!" Leo gazed at the monster before slowly walking towards it.

"Then why were you chasing me?" He said crossly.

"I was trying to apologise for scaring you," the monster snivelled. Fat tears dropped over his furry face, and dribble drizzled from his tusks, making him look sad and pathetic. Leo sat next to the monster.

"I'm sorry, I didn't mean to upset you. Here-" Leo stuck his hand out, "I'm Leo, I'd like to be your friend." The creature smiled as he shook Leo's hand.

"I'm Trevor, I'm a troll. I've always wanted a friend, but I'm too shy most of the time." Trevor smiled shyly and Leo beamed back at him.

Leo then realised that everyone is different, and he decided he would try to make more friends, because even trolls need someone to talk to.

LEO AND THE TERRIBLE TANTRUM

It was a bright and breezy day in Magic Forest as Leo and his new friend, Trevor the Troll, were busy making a house out of branches, twigs and leaves. Leo had been busy collecting armfuls of branches that looked good for making a roof for their house, and Trevor was digging a trench for a moat around the outside.

Trudging back through the forest to the house, Leo dropped to the ground the armful of branches and twigs he had collected, wiping his sweaty forehead onto his hoodie sleeve. Then he started to place the branches onto the roof, making sure he wouldn't knock any off.

When Trevor came to look at what Leo had done, he smiled and said, "that is wonderful, Leo. Now I'm going to go gather some flowers to decorate the roof!" Leo pulled a face, crossing his arms.

"I don't want silly flowers on the roof of *my* den! Flowers are for girls!" Trevor looked at his friend with a sad face.

"That's not a nice thing to say, Leo. Besides, *anyone* can like anything if they want to!" Leo stamped his foot in annoyance.

"*I* don't want to though. Aren't we *supposed* to be friends, making this den together?" Trevor stared at the floor before stepping forward towards Leo.

"I thought friends did things together. But *I* don't want to call it a den, I want it to be a *cave* but I didn't want to make you sad…" Trevor was starting to feel cross with

Leo because he did not feel that Leo was listening to him. A hot, itchy feeling started to tingle in Trevor's fingers and toes, he did not like being shouted at by his friend.

"You're just a..." Leo clenched his fists in anger, unable to stop the unkind words that flew out of his mouth, "a stinky troll! I'm *not* your friend!" With that, Trevor felt so cross and hurt, that he stood up as tall as he could and he gave out a huge:

"RRROOOAAARRR!"

Leo jumped back, afraid of what Trevor might do next. Trevor fell to the ground, surprised at himself as he was not normally someone who shouted at his friends, but Leo's hurtful words made him feel wobbly inside.

Bursting into tears, Trevor picked himself up and ran away, into the darkness of the forest. All the jolly birds had stopped singing and the forest echoed with Trevor's sobs as he howled.

Leo kicked a stone into the den, making a few twigs fall off the roof and he sat down on a log as he too began to cry. Leo cried quietly until a little voice sounded nearby.

"Hello, are you alright?" Leo opened his eyes, wiping his tears away quickly before looking at the person in front of him. Before him stood a little man, no larger than a pint glass and he had a large bushy beard and a wide brimmed blue hat that sat on top of his bushy eyebrows. He wore a pair of dungarees and black boots that made squishy sounds as he plodded in the mud towards Leo.

"Who...who are you?" Leo stammered. The little man pointed to himself, smiling.

"I'm Bingle, pleased to meet you! I'm a gnome!" Leo couldn't help but smile at Bingle's cheery face as they shook hands.

"I'm Leo," said Leo sadly. Bingle jumped onto the log next to Leo and patted his arm.

"You look sad, Leo. What's wrong?" Sighing, Leo told Bingle about the argument with Trevor and the small gnome nodded wisely.

"Now, I don't know what to do. I think I've lost my best friend!" Leo said, wiping his snotty nose on his sleeve as Bingle stood up on the log.

"You know, sometimes friends argue with each other. It's part of friendship. But it's how we can say sorry to each other that counts. Did you say something unkind to Trevor?" Bingle patted Leo's arm as the boy nodded.

"I did, and it's not true. I was just cross with him." Leo's voice was shaky with sadness as Bingle listened.

"Well, if you want Trevor to be your friend again then you have to say sorry. You need to try to think of how your words can upset other people, Leo. Until you apologise, Trevor won't want to be your friend." Leo nodded, rubbing his eyes.

"Let's go find Trevor," Bingle announced as he bounced from the log onto Leo's shoulder.

Standing, Leo went in search of his friend, following the wails and the sobs until they came across a small swamp. In the swamp lay Trevor, who was rolling around in the thick gooey mud, crying. He found the cool of the mud soothing when he felt sad.

Jumping to the ground, Bingle bounced onto a large red mushroom that stood tall enough for him to be seen by Trevor.

"Excuse me," Bingle squeaked and Trevor stopped rolling in the mud, staring at the tiny gnome. "Someone wants to say something to you," Bingle pointed towards Leo and Trevor frowned at him.

"I'm sorry Trevor, you're not stinky. That was unkind of me to say. And I *do* want to be your friend," Leo leaned forward to try to look into Trevor's eyes. "Please can we still be friends?" Trevor smacked the mud with a hand and said:

"What happens if you say it again? I thought you didn't like being my friend anymore. It really hurt my feelings." Leo shook his head.

"I promise I will never call you a name again. Friends don't call each other names. We might argue, but even best friends argue sometimes, and that's ok. We just have to talk about it afterwards." Trevor stood up and plopped his way through the mud before wrapping Leo in a big bear hug, mud flying everywhere.

Leo laughed, not minding that he was covered in thick gooey mud. The boy understood that even though sometimes people have problems, if they can talk and work through them it will help them to be a better person.

LEO AND THE WITCH OF THE WILDS

"Leo! Where are you?" Trevor called out, scratching his head as he peered into the thick of Magic Forest. They were playing hide-and-seek. "Leo?" Just as Trevor began to worry, a shape jumped out at him from the darkness.

"Boo!" It was Leo! He had wrapped some leaves around his head and he began to laugh. Trevor jumped and then laughed too when he saw his friend's smiling face.

"You scared me!" Trevor chuckled, as Leo began to do a silly dance on the spot, pulling funny faces. The two friends carried on their game of hide-and-seek and Trevor was feeling braver with each passing game until he wanted to be the one to hide.

Trevor ran with thundering steps into a garden that had a white picket fence that surrounded a small thatched cottage. The colours of the garden looked like a rainbow carpet, there were flowers that looked like bells which jingled softly in the breeze.

Trevor jumped behind a large shrub to hide, giggling to himself. He waited until he saw Leo walking towards the garden, and giggled with excitement.

Leo could not find Trevor, and it was at that moment he saw the thatched cottage. He ran towards the cottage and spied the large shrubbery. Realising that this was the only place Trevor could hide, Leo pounced around the shrub, shouting: "BOO!" Trevor jumped up, clapping his large, clawed hands.

"WHO are you?" A high-pitched voice cracked through the air behind Trevor and Leo, and they both whirled around on the spot.

The owner of the high-pitched voice was an old lady with glasses that settled on the bridge of her nose. Her long white hair was twisted into a plait and she wore a blue robe. She leant on a tall staff that held a large red stone, which glowed. She repeated herself:

"I said, who are *you*? And why are you in my garden? Get out!" She poked her staff at the pair, frowning at them. Leo ran through the white fence, but Trevor stumbled and fell over, squashing some of the grumpy old lady's bell-flowers. She shrieked.

"You'll pay for that! This garden has been perfect for hundreds of years!" She lifted both of her arms together, and suddenly, a glowing cage appeared around Trevor, trapping him. Trevor rattled the cage bars but lightning magic zapped his fingers, making him cry. Leo stared in horror as his friend was imprisoned by this grumpy old witch, and as she pointed her magic staff toward him, Leo fled.

Leo ran for quite some time, before stopping to catch his breath before he began to worry about Trevor. What would that witch do to him?

Leo began to pace up and down, feeling lost and frightened when a small squeaky voice piped up by his ear. Leo jumped in shock at the sight of the smallest girl he had ever seen, she had wings!

"Who are you?" Leo asked curiously. The small girl laughed and a tinkling sound could be heard before she responded.

"I'm Posie, I'm a fairy!" Posie sparkled, her bright wings hummed as she hovered in the air. "Why do you look sad?" Leo pointed back towards the thatched cottage.

"My friend has been captured by a witch! I don't know what to do!" Posie looked shocked before making a loud jingling sound. Just then, several more fairies appeared out from behind flowers and leaves within the forest. They all glittered and jingled as they flew to meet Leo, who gaped at the tiny creatures.

"We can help you, Leo!" The fairies chorused. Leo was stunned.

"How do you know my name?" He asked, puzzled. Posie smiled brightly.

"We hear everything in the forest, we have been making sure you are safe. We can help you by sending the Witch of the Wilds into a deep sleep." Leo looked excited and nodded.

"Then let's go save Trevor!"

Leo tiptoed back toward the cottage with the fairies flying behind him, and they saw Trevor still trapped in the cage. The witch sat in a rocking chair outside the pretty cottage. She knitted and hummed to herself in content before the fairies zoomed over to her, sprinkling her face with fairy dust.

The witch dropped her knitting and began to snore loudly as Leo dashed over to help Trevor. Leo tried to open the cage, but the lightning magic zapped him, so Leo looked around for something to use.

Posie pointed to the witch's staff.

"You can try undoing the magic with her staff, Leo!" She suggested. Leo ran over to the staff and grabbed it. He pointed it at his friend, shouting:

"Undo the magic!" A bolt of lightning shot from the staff at the enclosure, and the door fell open allowing Trevor to jump out. The two friends hugged and Leo remembered that he needed to deal with the witch's staff.

"Maybe you should break it, we don't want the Witch of the Wilds to do this to anyone else," Posie said. Leo looked at the witch who was fighting the sleep by trying to open her eyes and he shook his head.

"No, I can't break someone else's things. This staff might mean a lot to her." Leo carefully placed it back next to the witch who woke up and she snatched up her staff before holding it to her chest.

"My staff! You… didn't break it?" Leo shook his head at her question. She looked at Trevor with a sad expression.

"I don't have any friends who would risk their safety for me," She whispered, "thank you for not breaking my staff. I know now that I can't be horrible to people anymore.

I'm going to change my ways!" The witch had realised her mistake by trapping Trevor in the cage.

"It's ok," Leo said, "we can be your friends, if you promise not to do it again!" He laughed and the old lady laughed too, she wasn't grumpy anymore.

"I'm Opal," said the witch, shaking Leo's hand.

Leo realised right then, that no matter what a person might have done, they were still able to be good. Leo also understood that he was much braver than he realised he could be.

LEO AND THE WISHFUL WIZARD

One warm afternoon, Leo visited Magic Forest and came to see his friends: Trevor the troll and Bingle the Gnome. Leo was a very curious boy, and he wanted to know all about the magic in the forest.

"Where did the forest come from, Bingle?" Leo asked his friend. Bingle shrugged and squeaked in response.

"No one knows, it's a mystery! It has always been here, all of the magical folk heard about it and came through the magical door in the tree. Just like you did." Bingle jumped from red toadstool to toadstool, careful not to fall. Leo looked sadly at his hands.

"I wish I could do magic," the young boy said, "it looks like fun, and you all seem much happier here." Bingle patted his arm.

"But you can do so many things we can't, Leo. Like swinging off a tree branch! I'm far too short to do that!" Leo smiled as Bingle jumped onto his shoulder.

"Yes," agreed Trevor, "Leo, you can hide really well, I'm far too big to hide in small places like you can!" Trevor smiled at his friend, hoping he felt better.

Leo did feel better and the three friends carried on walking. Trevor picked wildflowers occasionally until they came upon a clearing in the forest with a tall stone tower in the middle. The tower had a large wooden door at the base, and Leo thought the tower looked like a lighthouse he had seen at the beach last summer.

Outside of the tower was a man with a long pointy beard. The man wore a long purple robe on top of a bright yellow shirt and baggy purple trousers with pointed slippers. He was a wizard, and he held a short wand in his hand which was creating some white sparks.

The wizard looked very cross and he shook the wand, shouting: "It's not working!"

The three friends stopped and Leo stepped forward to help.

"What's the matter? Do you need help?" The wizard held up his wand, frowning.

"My magic wand isn't working! I can't do any magic. I need someone to be my apprentice and I wanted to conjure a spirit to help me!" The wizard threw his magic wand on the ground as it sputtered sparks from the tip before he stamped on it.

Leo ran forward, worried that the wizard would break his wand.

"Don't break it, then you *really* won't be able to do any magic!" The wizard jumped up and down on the wand.

"Wands don't break! They're unbreakable! I'm just *very* angry!" The wizard's face was red as he shouted at the top of his lungs. "I'm *allowed* to be angry sometimes!"

Leo nodded in agreement. Leo then realised that even if he couldn't do magic, he could help others with their problems, and he really wanted to help the wizard.

"Of course, you can be angry sometimes, but you need to calm down in the end. Or you'll be angry forever and *never* get your magic to work." The wizard stopped, looking at the wise young boy before crossing his arms across his chest.

"I don't know how to calm down!" The wizard's face was still red as a tomato, "I feel cross *all* the time!" Leo pointed to a log on the ground, before sitting on it and tapped the log next to him for the wizard to join him.

"I can show you, if you'd like?" He asked the wizard, who nodded and sat next to him, his bushy beard bristling.

"First," Leo began, "put your hands on your knees, like this." He showed the wizard what to do by placing his hands on his own knees and the wizard copied Leo.

"Then, take a *deep* breath in, and slowly breathe out. Like this." Leo breathed in deeply, and then breathed out quickly. He repeated it over and over until the wizard began to copy his breathing.

Soon enough, the wizard's face turned from tomato red to his normal colour. The wizard smiled at Leo and nodded.

"Thank you, I feel *much* better!" The man picked up his wand, and as he breathed in deeply, a spark of warm yellow magic spurted smoothly out of the tip of the wand.

"What's your name?" Leo asked, sticking out his hand. The wizard shook it smiling.

"I am Edmund Evergreen and I've heard all about you, Leo." He gave the boy a knowing smile. Leo grinned as he saw Bingle stepping up to the wizard.

"I'd like to be your apprentice! To help you with your magic and your work. What do you think?" The wizard's face lit up in a huge smile before shaking Bingle's hand in agreement.

"Thank you, I am so happy you're offering to help. That is very kind!" Bingle bowed deeply and Leo clapped, laughing.

Just then, a wonderful thing happened. As Leo clapped his hands, sparks of magic shot out from his fingertips. He *could* do magic after all! Leo jumped in the air whooping for joy.

"I *can* do magic!" He cried jumping around like a ballerina. Trevor smiled and waved his arms in the air, feeling happy for his friend.

"See?" Trevor said, "It's because you did the deep breathing with Edmund! You can do anything if you put your mind to it, Leo! But remember, the magic will only work in the forest."

Leo smiled, and hugged his friends. Edmund joined in too and they all celebrated by jumping together in a group-hug.

Leo didn't mind that he couldn't do magic outside of Magic Forest, but he knew deep down that if he took his time with something then he could achieve whatever he wanted to. Especially if his friends were there for him.

LEO AND THE PASSIONATE PIXIE

One day, Leo was walking home from school, before he decided to take a shortcut towards the forest. He found the small wooden door and stepped through it before following the path toward where he might find Trevor the troll.

Finally, Leo found Trevor. He was making daisy chains in front of a fire by his favourite swamp, and when Leo called to him Trevor beamed at his best friend. They began to walk and Leo chatted about his day at school as Trevor listened carefully.

"What is a school?" Trevor asked Leo, inquisitively.

"It's a place where people go to learn stuff," Leo responded.

"Could I go to school?" Trevor looked puzzled as he scratched his head. Leo shrugged.

"You can't go to my school, but maybe a school here? In Magic Forest?" Trevor smiled and flapped his huge hands in excitement and he began to jump from foot to foot when suddenly, a small voice cried out:

"Hey! Watch where you're going!" Trevor stopped in his tracks, peering down to the ground. By his foot sat a tiny, grumpy girl. Her clothes were made of leaves. It was a pixie!

"Oh I'm very sorry," Trevor apologised, "I wasn't looking where I was going!" The pixie dusted herself off. She stood about as tall as a toadstool, and her fire-red hair shone in the light.

21

Leo smiled and crouched down to the ground, holding out a finger to her.

"Hello, I'm Leo. Who are you?" The pixie grasped Leo's finger and shook it firmly.

"I am Holly-" but before she could say anything else, Trevor interrupted.

"She's a pixie Leo! I've not seen pixie's around this part of Magic Forest for a long time!" Holly held her hands behind her back and nodded.

"Yes, we moved to Pixie Land on the other side of the forest, but I am on a quest!" Her eyes sparkled with excitement.

"Oh! Do go on!" Leo exclaimed.

"Well," Holly continued, "I am on a quest to learn to fly!" Leo made some 'oooh' sounds, but Trevor looked sad.

"But Holly," Trevor said gloomily, "pixies don't have wings, and you need wings to fly. Like the fairies." Holly sighed and plopped her head in her hands.

"Yes, I know. But I want to be different. Being a pixie is boring! Flying is so much more exciting!" Leo sat on a small patch of grass.

"Well, what's the difference between pixies and fairies?" Holly leant against a toadstool as she crossed her arms in front of her.

"Well, fairies have wings, they have fairy dust and they… fly. Pixie's are just… well we are very fast, so fast you can't see us zip around!" Holly showed Trevor and Leo her speed. Sure enough, Leo couldn't catch her if he blinked, she went: *zip zip zip*, from flower to flower, before suddenly appearing on Leo's shoulder, the boy grinned.

"That's so cool! You could pull some funny jokes on people." Holly shook her head.

"Nope, we don't do those things anymore. My grandfather used to play jokes on people all the time, not anymore though. What's the use of being super fast if you can't play?" She dangled her legs off Leo's shoulder, "life is so *boring*!" She moaned.

Leo opened his mouth to say something, but just then they all heard a cry.

"What's that?" Leo asked, worried. Holly's long ears listened and picked up the sound.

"Come on!" She shouted, "someone's in trouble, this way!" Holly led the three away through the shady trees and before long they came across a large bog. The bog smelt very bad, and was sticky. In the middle of the bog was a tiny man - it was a fairy! His wings were stuck in the boggy mud, and he was unable to move. His arms and legs were stuck in the brown gooey mess and he shouted at the top of his tiny lungs:

"HELP!" Leo looked around for something to use. There were no sticks long enough to reach to the middle of the bog, and so he looked for something to lie on. He found a large piece of tree bark and tried to lie on top of it, but he was too heavy and the bark snapped in half.

"I can't help!" Leo shouted back to the fairy, as he turned to Holly.

"Can you jump into the middle of the bog Holly?" The nervous pixie looked around nodding. She saw a large leaf hanging from a low tree branch. She zipped up the tree and snatched it up before jumping to the edge of the bog, laying the leaf carefully on the brown stickiness. The leaf was light enough to float on the top of the bog, and so she stepped onto it with a small stick. Holly was so small and light that the leaf held her weight, so she began to paddle the leaf across the bog with a stick.

When she was close enough, Holly did a running jump to the fairy, and with all her might she went: *zip zip zip* across the bog. She pulled the fairy out of the sticky mess as she managed to free him using her speed. Holly was too light for the bog to stick to her so she made it safely back to her leaf with the fairy.

Leo and Trevor cheered, jumping and punching the air with joy, as the fairy shook off as much of the gloop as he could before bowing low to Holly.

"Thank you, Miss Pixie, I will never forget your kindness," the fairy shook his wings before being able to fly back home to his fairy kingdom.

Holly paddled back to her new friends and laughed.

"See?" Leo said, shooting sparks from his fingertips, "you *can* do lots of things that others cannot do. Your super fast speed saved him!" Holly beamed brightly and nodded.

"You're right Leo, being fast is better than flying!" She danced around with her friends, glad that she finally felt important.

LEO AND GNASHER THE GNARLED

Leo was rushing his homework, so he could go and find his friends in Magic Forest. It was a warm and sunny Saturday afternoon and soon he was free, running down the familiar path and stepping through the tree-door into the magical forest.

He ran towards Trevor's cave, which was his home, and knocked on the huge wooden door. Trevor did not answer the door, so Leo poked his head around as he opened it. Before him he could see Trevor's furniture and bookcase lying across the floor.

Trevor's cave-home was always tidy, so seeing Trevor's armchair broken and lying across the cave floor worried Leo. Everything was a mess and there was no note that Trevor may have left behind.

Just then, Holly's little pixie voice rang out behind Leo.

"Leo! Trevor's been kidnapped!" Leo spun around on the spot.

"What? Where is he?" the small pixie pointed back towards the front door.

"He has been taken to the arena, to fight!" Holly was biting her nails as Leo ran past her, she zipped ahead of him to show him the way to the arena.

They both ran North away from Trevor's cave before finding a huge arena where some of Magic Forest's trees had been ripped out of the ground. The arena had lights surrounding it that shone brightly and a huge gate blocked Leo from entering.

Leo and Holly peered in through the bars of the gate, they could see several cages with different woodland creatures trapped inside and the biggest cage held:

"Trevor!" Leo cried out when he saw his friend. Trevor sat in a corner of the pen crying into his big hands. "I must *do* something!" Leo looked around for some way in, but realised that the only way through was to take part of the arena.

"What is this arena Holly?" Leo crouched down to hear his small friend's voice.

"People fight in the arena, until they can't fight anymore!" Her voice squeaked.

"I need to take Trevor's place," Leo said firmly. Holly squeaked in shock.

"You won't win! You surely will lose Leo!" The boy sighed looking back at Trevor, realising that he felt scared for his friend more than for himself.

"I must try to help Trevor." Just then, a side gate opened and out came a huge lumbering troll. He was three times as big as Trevor, and he held a huge club in his hands. His face turned into a sneer, elephant-sized tusks stuck out from his mouth and he stomped around the arena laughing at the creatures in the enclosures.

"I am Gnasher: The Gnarled! No one can defeat me!" The great troll bellowed. He laughed at Trevor as the small troll wailed in fright in his cage. Gnasher bashed his own chest, letting out a great big burp of a roar.

Leo saw the Arena Master with a long black coat standing at the gate so he ran towards the man. Holly jumped onto Leo's shoulder whispering advice into his ear.

"Use his size against him, Leo." Leo nodded before walking right up to the Arena Master.

"Excuse me," he shouted as fiercely as he could, "I'd like to take Trevor's place. You can have me instead." The Arena Master looked Leo up and down, laughing before nodding.

"Alright, in you go!" He pushed Leo into the arena and Holly zipped past the gate, ready to help her friend.

"Hey!" Leo bellowed at Gnasher, "Why don't you come and pick on someone else, you big bully!" Gnasher's great, thick head turned toward Leo and he let out a roar of a laugh before taking a running-jump towards him.

Now, Leo was much smaller, and faster than Gnasher, so he could outmanoeuvre him. Leo jumped and rolled to one side as Gnasher stumbled past him, smashing into the arena stone wall. Shaking his head, Gnasher ran at Leo again. Leo swiftly stepped to one side again and Holly whooped. The crowd in the stands cheered as the giant troll tripped and fell.

The gigantic creature ran at Leo several more times, before he let exhaustion overcome him, and the beast sat on the ground to catch his breath. Leo didn't need to hurt the troll at all, the brute was doing all the hard work for him. A sudden feeling of bravery welled up inside Leo and he ran towards the cages with Holly. She managed to climb inside one of the padlocks of the enclosures and began to undo the lock.

Leo gambolled away as Gnasher ran at him again and again, continually hurting himself as he tripped and fell or crashed into the arena wall. Holly undid all the cage locks just as Gnasher did one last tumble. It was then that Gnasher could not get up, and he held his head groaning.

"Ahhhh!" he roared, "I cannot go on! I surrender!" The crowd cheered for Leo, and Trevor burst out of his unlocked cage, lifting Leo high up in the air. Leo and Holly were both heroes and the crowd chanted: "Leo! Holly!" As the pair were celebrated.

"Leo is the winner!" The Arena Master called out to everyone. Leo stepped towards the Arena Master with his arms crossed.

"You need to stop taking people against their will to fight, it's not kind or ethical. Otherwise my friends and I will just release them all each time!" The Arena Master nodded in defeat as he held up his hands.

"Alright, the Arena Games will only *ask* people to join, we will not *force* anyone to do anything against their will *ever* again!

Leo shook hands with the arena master, and then turned back to his cheering friends.

"Leo!" Trevor called to him, "you were so brave!" Leo smiled. He had felt very frightened while in the arena, but he knew that because he was calm, he was able to think clearly. Gnasher had been too angry to be able to think clearly, and Leo knew that if he kept his cool, he was sure to win anything.

LEO AND THE BOASTFUL BIGFOOT

One day, Leo and Trevor were helping the gnome community to build some new tree houses in Magic Forest. Together the boy, troll and all the fairy-folk were busy gathering wood, cutting logs and collecting moss for water-proofing the tree houses. Other magical creatures were coming from all over the forest. Fairies were helping too, by flying from tree to tree dropping off sticks and string for the tree houses and Holly's pixie family were helping gather moss from far away, zipping back in no time.

Soon, a large figure stepped through the busy crowd. He was a Bigfoot! He had long fur covering his body and he stood tall enough to reach the tree houses. His feet were massive in size.

Leo saw the newcomer and excitedly skipped up to him.

"Hello!" Leo said waving, "I'm Leo! What's your name?" The Bigfoot grinned and opened up furry arms.

"I am Bert, I just thought I'd come to see what you're doing." Bert stood with his hands on his hips looking around at everyone.

"Well actually," Leo said pointing to the gnomes cutting logs, "we do need another pair of hands to help out! Just go over there and the gnomes will tell you what they need you to do. Thank you so much!" And with that Leo skipped back to his own job.

Bert the Bigfoot looked around lazily, giving a huge yawn before walking over to where Leo pointed. He sat down to lean against a tree and stuck a long piece of grass in his mouth before closing his eyes to sleep.

The gnomes tried to work around the sleeping Bigfoot, but he was in the way so they had to wake him up after a few minutes. When Bert awoke, the gnomes asked him to pass some tools to them which he did, but he moaned:

"I'm not used to this type of work, you know. I am more of a brainy person." He tapped his head and smirked to everyone. The gnomes looked very puzzled.

"You know, I am the leader of the Bigfoot committee. I have lots of hard thinking to do." The vain creature boasted. Holly stamped her feet as she stormed over to the Bigfoot.

"Well, do you *think* you could help us here then?" She tapped her toes on the ground impatiently.

"Oh no!" Bert exclaimed, "I'm not made for working hard. Just hard thinking." The gnomes began to grumble to each other as they tried to keep working around the boastful creature. He refused to move as he was worried about getting dirty with the work and ruining his clean fur.

After a while Leo noticed that Bert was not helping, so he walked over to him to ask him what he was doing.

"I thought you came to help us?" Leo asked, crossing his arms in front of him. Bert shook his head.

"No, I'm not that kind of worker. I just like to watch. I'm excellent at observing, you know." Leo stamped his foot and frowned at the idle Bigfoot.

"If you're going to just be lazy then go away! We don't need you lying around here, bragging about what *you* want to do!" Leo was so cross he lifted his arms in the air and it was just then that the Bigfoot began to cry.

"Why is everyone being horrid to me?" He wailed, fat tears dropping down his clean fur. "I just wanted to make some friends!"

Leo sighed and patted the Bigfoot on his arm.

"I'm sorry I shouted at you, but you're in the way." Bert rubbed his furry face.

"But I can't help because I'm not strong at all. Or good at making tree houses. Or good at anything!" The gnomes gathered around the weeping Bigfoot as the truth unraveled.

"It's ok," Holly said reassuringly as she zipped to Leo's shoulder, "you don't have to be good at everything. But if you try *one* thing, you might find you are good at it!" The Bigfoot nodded and stood up. Telling the truth felt a lot better than he thought it might. Bert helped the gnomes lift a log with some rope, and he was able to lift it high above his head as he placed it in a tree house.

Everyone cheered and Bert was so pleased he managed to help.

"You *can* do things, when you put your mind to it!" Leo said. "It's more important to have a kind heart and try to help others. Today you have helped the fairy-folk with their tree houses so they can live in them!" Leo smiled at Bert who stood back grinning.

"Yes! You're right, Leo. I'm sorry about before." Leo shrugged, creating a hot chocolate for Bert with his magic.

"That's ok, friends can always make up after a good chat." And with that, they got back to work.

LEO AND THE FALLEN FAUN

Today is the perfect day to go fishing at the forest lake, Leo thought as he and his new magical friends dangled their legs over the side of the boardwalk with wooden fishing rods that bobbed in the calm waters. Magic Forest surrounded the huge lake on all sides, and the sound of his friends talking and laughing made Leo smile.

Leo's friends were all very interested in Leo's life at home, which he would think was very boring. They all thought it sounded fresh and exciting, because they had never crossed through the tree-door before into the non-magical world.

Trevor had made some ham and cheese sandwiches, and was offering them around to the group. The pixies and fairies loved the crisps, but the gnomes gobbled down the tasty sandwiches.

Just as Leo was chewing on his sandwich, the group heard a girl scream from inside the forest. The friends all jumped up in alarm before laying down their fishing rods, running towards the scream. Trevor was the last to follow, feeling scared as the scream sounded very close by.

Leo ran until he found a shape lying in a tangle of stinging nettles on the ground.

It was a faun!

Leo rushed to her side asking if she was badly hurt.

"What can I do to help?" Leo asked. The delicate creature pointed to her ankle. Her two legs and feet were the shape of goat legs and hooves, her blonde speckled fur soft to the touch. Leo noticed her hoof was tangled up in the large tree root that stuck out from the ground.

"My ankle," she cried, tear globules dripped down her speckly face, "it hurts so much!" Leo noticed that the root of the tree held fast onto her ankle, no matter what he tried to do it would not budge.

"Come one everyone," Leo called to his friends, "let's do this together!" Everyone clambered around to help, trying to free the faun's hoof.

The gnomes were strong enough to try to lift the tree root slightly, while the fairies sprinkled her ankle with fairy dust and the pixies used their speed to yank the faun's ankle from underneath the tree root. Trevor patted the faun's hand and Leo talked to her to distract her.

Finally, with one big push, the pixies shoved the hoof and the young faun was free! She smiled and shakily stood up, but found that she was unable to stand at all, so she flopped to the ground.

"What do I do now?" she sighed.

"Maybe we can make you a stretcher?" Leo suggested. His friends looked baffled.

"What's a stretcher, Leo?" Holly piped up.

"Well, it's a bed that can be moved around for when people get too ill to travel. Here, look." Leo drew in the dirt path the outline of a stretcher and everyone nodded.

"Ok then," Trevor announced, "Let's do this. Then we can take this young lady to the healer!" Everyone agreed, and they all hunted for strong tree branches they could lash together. Large leaves were used to create the bed of the stretcher and soon the faun clambered into it, very grateful.

"Oh thank you so much!" She breathed as Leo and Trevor picked up the stretcher between them. "I don't know how I can repay you!" Leo grinned and called over his shoulder:

"Just tell us your name!" The faun smiled.

"Flora, my name is Flora." Leo smiled, he and his friends plodding onwards.

Just then, Flora's large ears, which poked out from her blonde hair on top of her head, swivelled around like cat ears. She bolted upright on the stretcher.

"There's something dangerous nearby!" She whispered in fear. Everyone stopped and Leo and Trevor gently placed the stretcher down.

Sure enough, lumbering from the darkness of the forest came a great big grizzly bear! The bear saw the group and stood on its hind legs, paws clawing the air.

"AHHHHHHH!" Trevor cried out in fright as he dashed behind a boulder. Leo was scared too, but he called the fairies to help him.

"Can you sprinkle fairy dust on him, to make him sleep?" The bear took a couple of steps towards the scared group, as the fairies nodded. "Quickly!" Leo cried.

The fairies flew towards the bear as it swiped at them, but they dodged its attack. Sprinkling their fairy dust over the bear, it fell to the ground in a sleeping position, nestling its wet black nose into its paws as sleep came over it.

"Phew!" Trevor said, peeping out from behind the boulder, "that was close!" Leo agreed, and soon everyone was setting off towards the healer's house with Flora on the stretcher.

When they arrived, the healer was outside her home, pegging her laundry on the washing line.

When she saw Flora, she ushered in Leo and Trevor who held Flora carefully as they guided her into the healer's hut. When she was settled on the healer's bed, Flora began to cry.

"Does it hurt very much?" Leo asked, patting her hand. Flora shook her head.

"It's not that, it's just… when I fell I broke my flute…" She held up a wooden flute that had snapped in half.

"Let me try to help with that," Leo said, smiling. Flora passed him the broken flute and he stepped outside to his friends.

Once he had told his friends about Flora's broken flute, the gnomes immediately got to work creating a new flute for Flora, making sure it was exactly the same. An hour went by, and Leo held up the new flute, thanking his friends.

He walked back into the healer's hut and gave Flora the new flute, her face brightened into a smile.

"Oh thank you, Leo!" She said, giving him a kiss on his cheek. Leo blushed and shrugged.

"It was all of us, not just me," Leo said, he knew that was the right thing to say. He knew that if it had not been for his friends, he would not have been able to make the flute on his own, nor make the stretcher. Leo was so grateful for his friends being there for him.

LEO AND THE GOADING GOBLIN

"Higher Leo, higher!" Flora called out as she was swung high into the trees on the makeshift swing that Leo had made for her. The boy laughed as he pushed as hard as he could, the swing whistling through the air. Leo wanted to make the swing more fun for Flora, so he created with his magic a small rabbit to climb into the air and jump around her, making her laugh. The magic then sparkled and exploded like a firework making Trevor go: "ooohhhh" as droplets of magic tickled his nose.

Flora climbed off the swing and clapped her hands.

"Do some more magic, Leo!" She pranced from hoof to hoof, dancing around Trevor. Leo pointed his fingers towards the trees, imagining the leaves were pink. Sparkles spat out from the tips of Leo's fingers, and the leaves of the tree in front of him slowly turned a pale pink colour. Trevor laughed, picking a large leaf from the tree, watching as it slowly faded back to a normal green colour.

"I love doing magic here! It feels wonderful!" Leo said smiling. He sat on the grassy bank as Flora began to play her musical flute. Enjoying the music, Trevor began to sing along to the tune.

Just then the three friends heard a grumbling coming down the dirt path and soon enough, they saw a small green goblin, with a long pointed nose and a red cap on his head. Leo smiled and was about to say hello to the goblin when he jumped as he saw them.

"A human! In the forest?" The goblin shouted at the three of them, pointing at Leo. "What's he *doing* here? He doesn't *belong* here! He's not magical!" Flora stopped playing her flute and put her hands on her hips. She looked very cross.

"That is a really unkind thing to say. This is our friend, Leo. He has helped many magical folk in Magic Forest!" The goblin waddled over, wiping his snotty nose onto a grubby arm.

"He's human," he hissed, "human's smell really awful. I knew something was not right when I began to walk this way!" The goblin's unkind words hurt Leo's feelings and Leo frowned.

"Hey!" The boy accidentally shot magic sparks from his fingers, "I *can* do magic, and also, *anyone* can come to Magic Forest!" The goblin laughed at Leo, making him feel small before spluttered and coughing, as if he had a cold.

"Humans! Do magic! Bah-aha! Nonsense! You're not any good at magic!" Leo growled at the goblin's nasty words.

"Look here…" The frustrated boy stopped, realising he did not know the goblin's name. The creature quickly said:

"Snot is the name," Leo nodded, still frowning.

"Listen here *Snot*, I help these fairy-folk and woodland creatures and *they* say I can be here." Flora and Trevor both nodded, but Trevor looked worried at the goblin.

"Humans are stinky! They're good-for-nothing, and mean to us fairy-folk," Snot continued. Leo stood back, as tears started to form in his eyes. He had never had anyone say such awful things to him, not even at school, and he fell to his knees as the tears flowed over his face. Leo did not like being bullied, because it made him feel sad. Snot just jumped closer towards him, laughing in his face.

"Stinky human!" He sang, "useless, boring, smelly human!" Flora felt so cross with the unkind words, that she pawed the ground with her hoof and charged at Snot, her small horns tossing him high in the air.

Snot gave out an almighty yelp as he flew through the air, before bouncing to the ground onto his bottom. Rubbing his sore behind, the goblin clambered to his feet.

Before he could grumble anything more, Flora charged at him again which made him run away so fast that his red cap blew off his head. Snot ran, squealing like a piglet and soon, he was gone.

Flora turned to Leo, who sat with his head in his hands, crying. Trevor patted his back trying to soothe him and Flora gave Leo a big hug.

"Hugs make me feel better when I'm sad," Flora said, squeezing Leo tight. Leo sighed and the tears stopped.

"Thank you Flora, thank you Trevor. I just don't understand why Snot would be so mean?" He asked them. Flora sighed and looked at Leo.

"Sometimes people get jealous of what they do not have. Goblins do not have any magic at all," Leo was surprised at her words. Flora smiled nodding, "yes, I think Snot was jealous of you Leo. Magic is special, and *can* be used in any way that is safe. You should feel proud of yourself. *You* can do something that not many people can." Leo sat up straight as he wiped his face dry.

"Yes, I do feel a little proud. I can feel the magic here, in the air and in the ground. It's a wonderful feeling to be able to control it!"

Just then, Leo felt a gentle tap on his shoulder and he turned to see one of the forest trees bowing down to him. The tree held a small stick that had special carvings, which decorated the side of the stick.

"What's this?" Leo asked the tree, taking the sturdy twig. The tree said nothing, for trees cannot talk, but Flora clapped her hands excitedly.

"It's a wand, Leo! The forest has given you your very own wand! That is so wonderful. Now your magic can flow!" Leo smiled, the adventurous feeling building up inside of him once again. He tilted the wand, and instead of the magic spurting out, it flowed out from the tip of the wand smoothly, like water in a river.

Leo felt encouraged by his magic abilities and his wand. The wise boy knew he would try to ignore people who said nasty and unkind things. He knew what was right and what he wanted to do. Leo promised to himself that no one else would be able to upset him like that ever again, because only *he* knew how special he was.

LEO AND DRAKE THE DRAGON

A few days passed by since Leo's last visit to Magic Forest, then the days rolled into a week before Leo could visit his magical friends again.

One hot summer's day, Leo managed to slip away from the watchful gaze of his parents, and crept into the wood. When he saw the familiar tree-door, he began to run with the excitement of seeing all of his magical friends again. The tree-door opened easily, as it always did, and as Leo stepped under the cool canopy of Magic Forest, he nearly crashed into Bungle. The little gnome sat on a tree stump and as soon as he saw Leo enter through the tree-door he jumped up, his hands worrying around the conical point of his hat.

"Bungle!" Leo exclaimed, smiling. "You made me jump!" Leo bent down to shake the small gnome's hand but the gnome gripped his finger looking as though he were about to burst into tears.

"Leo, a terrible thing has happened! You must come with me at once!" Bungle grabbed Leo's thumb and began to tug him along the dirt path. Suddenly worried, Leo tried to ask what was wrong, but Bungle kept stuttering until he began to mumble under his breath.

The pair walked deep into the forest, and soon enough, they came upon a huge castle that Leo guessed was in the heart of the forest. The trees exposed the sky, but the colour wasn't the bright blue that Leo had seen back at home. Here, the sky was a deep purple and dark clouds swirled high above the tallest tower on the castle. Thunder sounded, and Leo took a step back, frightened.

"What is this place?" He uttered. Just then, Leo heard voices chattering in the distance, not too far away. He followed them with a timid Bungle following close by. Leo found the source of the voices: it was the forest creatures, and Trevor was there. When all the creatures saw Leo they cried out and ran to him. Trevor bounded up to Leo.

"Leo, Flora was taken!" Startled, Leo gasped at the announcement. Trevor continued. "The keeper of this castle is a terrifying dragon - he took her! We are so worried that he'll eat her! What do we do?" Clenching his fists, Leo looked at the castle. It towered high above them as the clever boy began to devise a plan.

"Everyone!" Leo called out, lowering his hands, "I need you all to listen to me… I have a plan."

A moment later, the magical creatures understood what they had to do from Leo's instructions, and they all set off towards the castle. Approaching the huge building, the fairies sprinkled their fairy dust onto the creatures who couldn't fly, and the creatures rose into the air. Leo stayed on the ground with Trevor, marching up to the huge wooden entrance door to the castle. Trevor banged on the door with all his troll strength, the sound echoing before a roar sounded.

A thudding smashed across the ground as the two brave friends felt the dragon's steps vibrate as he came closer and closer.

Just then, the wooden door banged open with a mighty *CRASH* and Trevor and Leo fell backwards. The dragon before them was huge and was covered in glittering green scales. His bright red eyes glinted in the storm above and he lowered his snout towards them, taking in giant sniffs.

Then, the strangest thing happened.

The dragon sat back on its haunches and… *smiled*. Leo frowned before standing up, helping Trevor to his feet.

"You have our friend, let her go!" Leo shouted at the dragon. The dragon looked surprised before he answered.

"But we were having a nice spot of tea!" The dragon's voice sounded very polite. Leo called up to the beast in response:

"If you eat her, there'll be trouble!" Leo looked around for his magical friends before shouting: "NOW!" As he gave the command, the fairies appeared above the dragon's head, sprinkling fairy dust into his eyes to make him sleep. The other flying creatures held a chain that was attached to a collar around the dragon's neck and everyone flew around the dragon to tie him up. The plan worked, all the creatures pulled the chain, and the dragon fell to his knees. However, the giant lizard wasn't affected by the fairy dust. Suddenly, he began to cry.

"Ohhh! Please don't hurt me! I wasn't going to eat her! I just wanted a friend!" As the dragon sobbed, Flora appeared from behind the beast's slumped figure.

"Leo! Stop!" She called, holding her hands up as she ran towards Leo and his friends.

"This is Drake, he is trapped here in this castle, he took me because he was lonely." She turned to the dragon in a scolding manner. "He *should* have asked me if I wanted to go with him, but I understand now that he's not dangerous." Leo ran to Flora, hugging her tightly.

"At least you're ok Flora!" He smiled. Turning to Drake, Leo apologised. "I'm sorry Drake, I just assumed that you were going to hurt her because you're a dragon." Drake let a fat tear splodge to the ground with a *thud*.

"Not all dragons are the same, you know." He replied as the creatures released him. Flora clapped her hands.

"I know!" She said animatedly, "we can let Drake go, let's get that collar off so you're free!" With a lot of effort from the fairy's magic, and strength from Trevor, Leo and his friends undid the dragon's collar, letting it clank to the floor. The dragon shook his head.

"Oh thank you so much! I am free at last!" Leo smiled.

"Well, without my friends' help and Flora's understanding we wouldn't have been able to help you, Drake. I'd like to visit you each week, if that's ok?" The giant beast nodded, stretching his papery wings out either side of him before taking flight.

Leo and his friends watched as Drake swooped out of sight. The boy had learnt that he shouldn't judge others, because of things they have done, or who they appear to be, but look forward to the wonderful things they can do.

Leo hugged his friends, grateful for their help in Drake's rescue, he would have never been able to release Drake without his friends.

DISCLAIMER

This book contains opinions and ideas of the author and is meant to teach the reader informative and helpful knowledge while due care should be taken by the user in the application of the information provided. The instructions and strategies are possibly not right for every reader and there is no guarantee that they work for everyone. Using this book and implementing the information/recipes therein contained is explicitly your own responsibility and risk. This work with all its contents, does not guarantee correctness, completion, quality or correctness of the provided information. Misinformation or misprints cannot be completely eliminated.

Printed in Great Britain
by Amazon